margaret Tempest.

HOW
LITTLE GREY RABBIT
GOT BACK HER TAIL.

BY ALISON UTTLEY
PICTURES BY
MARGARET TEMPEST

LONDON: WILLIAM HEINEMANN LTD.

HOW LITTLE GREY RABBIT GOT BACK HER TAIL

ONE COLD MARCH MORNING little Grey Rabbit awoke at dawn for this was to be a busy day.

Softly she opened her door and listened. Snores could be heard coming from Hare's room, and squeaky little grunts from Squirrel's.

She crept downstairs, took down a round wicker basket and then went out into the raw air.

THE SUN HAD NOT RISEN, AND A star was still in the sky, "like a candle for a little rabbit," she thought.

As she walked down the garden path she looked back at the shut windows, and waved a paw to her sleeping friends in the little house.

She turned down the lane and scampered over the stones, leaping over thorny briars, and swinging her basket round and round over her head.

A STARTLED MOUSE GAZED AFTER her. "I wonder where she is going? It's a pity she's lost her tail, she must feel cold. They say it is fastened up on Wise Owl's door, but may I never see it!"

Grey Rabbit came to an opening in a hedge, and climbed through, tearing her apron on a curved thorn.

She stopped to pin it with a straight pin from a hawthorn bush, and to sip the water from a gurgling spring, like a small fountain in the grass.

THEN SHE RAN ACROSS THE WET
meadow to a bank where the first
primroses were growing. She put down
her basket and began to pick them,
biting off their pink stalks, and putting
the yellow blossoms in the basket.

When she finished there, she ran to
another field, and another, and another,
with a basket now heaped with petals.
Behind her she left a trail of small

footprints which scarcely pressed down the grey-green grass.

Suddenly a black nose and two pink hands with funny little human fingers stuck out of the earth in front of her. She started back.

"Oh! Oh! Moldy Warp, how you frightened me!" she exclaimed, with her paw on her fluttering heart. "Wherever have you come from?"

"I WAS ASLEEP, GREY RABBIT, BUT you woke me, so I came out to see who it was," and the Mole shook off the red soil clinging to his bare feet and wiped his hands on the grass.

"What are you doing out here so early, Grey Rabbit?"

"I am picking primroses for Primrose Wine," answered the Rabbit. "Hare has a bad cold and it's a certain cure. My mother used to make it."

"What a clever Rabbit you are!" said the Mole admiringly. "But where is your tail?" he added, blinking his small eyes.

GREY RABBIT TOLD HOW SHE gave her tail to Wise Owl in return for his advice on gardening.

"I didn't know Owl was a gardener," said Moldy Warp shortly. "I thought I was the best digger hereabouts."

"Of course you are, Moldy; there is no one like you except Badger. Owl told me about seeds, carrot seed, and lettuce seed."

"Oh! He did, did he?" muttered the Mole; "and he took your tail, did he?"

"No, I gave it to him," returned Grey Rabbit sadly.

"GREY RABBIT," SAID THE MOLE
solemnly, "would you like your
tail back, very very much?"

"Very very much," answered Grey
Rabbit mournfully, "but Owl is a kind of
friend, and he must not be made my
enemy."

"I'll help you, Grey Rabbit," said the
Mole, striking his breast with his hand,

just as a long level sunray shone across the field and turned his velvet waistcoat red. "I will think out a plan and we will get it back."

"Good-bye, and thank you, Moldy Warp," said the Rabbit. "I must run now, or I shall be late for breakfast," and off she ran with her flowers bobbing up and down in the basket.

AT THE LITTLE HOUSE BY THE Wood, there was dismay when Grey Rabbit was missed. Hare ran up and downstairs with his head in a red cotton handkerchief, calling, "Where are you, Grey Rabbit? A-tishoo! Are you hiding, Grey Rabbit? A-tishoo!"

B UT SQUIRREL SAW THE BASKET
was gone, and guessed the Rabbit
was busy somewhere.

"Help me to get the breakfast, Hare,
instead of calling like that," she scolded.

Hare wiped his eyes and sneezed violently. "A-tishoo! A-tishoo!" went he,
and he swept the tablecloth off the table
and wrapped it round his shoulders.

"Oh, do be careful!" exclaimed Squirrel, indignantly seizing the cloth and
shaking it.

SHE RESET THE TABLE, MADE A dish of scrambled ants' eggs, and drew up the chairs.

"Rat-a-tat-tat" came Hedgehog with the milk.

"Late again! Have you seen Grey Rabbit?" asked Squirrel.

Hedgehog shook his old head. "No," said he, "I've been too busy a-milking my cow. She wouldn't lie still this morning, and I had to chase her all over the field. Is Little Grey Rabbit missing?"

"Of course she is or I should not ask you," snapped the Squirrel.

"Sorry, no offence," said the Hedgehog, picking up his milkcan.

"I can't abide that pair," he muttered. "Now, Little Grey Rabbit is a nice little thing."

A light footstep came up the lane and a voice was heard singing:

"Primroses, Primroses,
   Primroses fine,
   Pick them and press them,
   And make yellow wine."

THE GREY RABBIT TRIPPED UP to him. "Good-morning, Hedgehog. Have you brought the milk?"

"Yes, and had my head snapped off by those two. They think another Weasel has you," and he laughed grimly.

She opened the gate and ran to the house.

"Hare! Squirrel! Look at my primroses, a basketful, picked with the dew on them, to make Primrose Wine and cure your cold, Hare!"

ALL DAY THEY MADE THE WINE. Grey Rabbit packed the heads in layers in a wooden cask, tightly, and between each layer she put an acorn-cup of honey and a squeeze of wood-sorrel juice.

Squirrel filled the kettle many times from the brook, and put it on the fire. Grey Rabbit poured the boiling water over the flowers until the cask was full. Then she sealed it with melted bees-wax and buried it in the garden.

"HOW TIRED I AM," SAID HARE, AS they sat down to tea.

"How tired I am," said Squirrel.

"How glad I am the wine is made," said Grey Rabbit, as she poured out the tea and cut the bread and carrot.

"When can we have some?" asked Hare.

"In twenty-four hours," said the Rabbit, and Hare began to count the minutes, and to sneeze very loudly.

That night Wise Owl flew over the house.

"TOO-WHIT, A-TISHOO! TOO-whoo, A-tishoo!" he cried. "Too-Wishoo-oo-oo! Too-Whoosh-oo-oo!"

As he flew far over fields and woods there came a faint Tishoo-oo-oo floating in the wind.

"Poor Wise Owl," murmured Grey Rabbit to her blanket, "I must take him a bottle of Primrose Wine, too.''

The next day Squirrel, dressed in a brown overall, worked in the garden, digging the soil, and sowing fresh dandelion and lettuce seed.

Hare sat sneezing by the fire, playing noughts and crosses against himself. He always won, so he was happy.

GREY RABBIT HAD SOME SEWING to do. She sat in the rocking-chair mending her torn apron. Her needle ran in and out, and the tiny bobbins of cotton emptied themselves as she sewed.

At last she finished and put away her work. Squirrel came in, stamping her feet and crying out against the cold.

"It's bitter to-day, Grey Rabbit. Where's my teazle brush? It's time you got me another."

Grey Rabbit found the brush in the wood-scuttle, where Squirrel had thrown it.

SHE BRUSHED AND COMBED THE Squirrel's tail until it was glossy and bright again.

After dinner she left Hare explaining how to win at noughts and crosses to Squirrel, who could never understand, and away she went over the brook and through the Wood with her basket.

The trees were bare, but here and there a honeysuckle waved tender green leaves as it climbed up a nut-tree. The Rabbit stopped to look longingly at a horse-chestnut whose sticky buds were beyond her reach.

"IF ONLY SQUIRREL WOULD COME in the Wood again," said she, "we could have such delicious meals!"

It was very quiet; no rabbits ran among the undergrowth, no birds sang in the tree-tops, only now and then a rook flew overhead, or a pheasant scattered the beech-leaves which covered the ground. The Rabbit's heart thumped, she was always nervous in this Wood. Her ears were pressed back and her eyes looked all ways at once, but nothing came to alarm her.

At last she ran through the gate and entered the Teazle-field. She bit off a few heads, all dry and prickly, and then she filled her basket with curling shoots of young green bracken, which she found hidden under the dead-gold fronds.

Home she ran, softly through the Wood, stepping on the soft moss and mould, and avoiding the rustling leaves.

"Robin Redbreast has been with a letter for you," said Squirrel, emptying the basket in the larder and putting the brushes in a cupboard.

GREY RABBIT TOOK THE tightly-sealed leaf-envelope, and broke open the brown flap.

"Who is it from?" asked the curious Hare.

"It's Moldy Warp's writing," answered Rabbit, as she turned the letter up and down, inside and out.

"What does it say?" asked Squirrel.

"It says 'Found Knock Mole,'" said Rabbit.

"Whatever can it mean?" they all asked.

HARE SAID, "MOLDY WARP HAS been found knocked over."

Squirrel said, "Mr Knock has found Mole."

Grey Rabbit said, "Mole has found a Knock, but who has lost one?"

As the evening wore on Hare got more and more excited, until he could hardly bear to wait for Rabbit to dig up the cask.

The seals were broken and such a delicious smell came into the room, like pine forests, and honeysuckle, and lime-trees in flower.

Grey Rabbit filled a bottle and tucked it under her arm. "I'm going off at once with this bottle to Wise Owl," said she.

It was a dark night, and the Wood was full of little sounds, rustles and murmurs. Grey Rabbit felt very frightened, for they were not comfortable homely sounds and she looked up at the blinking stars.

"A-tishoo! A-tishoo! Tishoo!" came echoing through the trees, and she caught sight of Owl's shining eyes, and her own little white tail hanging on the door of the oak tree.

"WISE OWL, I'VE BROUGHT YOU some Primrose Wine for your sneeze," said she.

"Thank you, Grey Rabbit, thank you kindly. Even old Owl could not make Primrose Wine. What would you like, Grey Rabbit?"

She hesitated and looked at her tail.

"No, Grey Rabbit, I could not part with that, unless you bring me a bell to go Ting-a-ling-a-ling when visitors call. But here is a book of riddles."

"But, Wise Owl, where shall I find a bell?" said poor Grey Rabbit, who sadly wanted her tail.

GREY RABBIT RAN HOME AGAIN with the book in her paw, but her thoughts full of the bell.

Squirrel and Hare were sitting up for her, and between them, sipping from a tea-cup, sat the Mole.

"Here she comes! Here she comes!" they cried, as the latch rattled and she flung open the door.

"Mole has something for you," said Hare excitedly.

Mole brought out a large silver penny, with an eagle on one side and an emperor on the other.

"IT'S ROMAN," HE SAID. "I thought it would do for Wise Owl's door-knocker."

"Oh, you kind Moldy Warp! Do you mean instead of my tail? Alas! Wise Owl will only give it to me for a bell."

"A bell? Where can we get a bell?"

"A bell rings people to Church," said Hare.

"There is a bell in the village shop," said Grey Rabbit.

"A bell calls the children to school," said Squirrel.

"There are Hare-bells, Blue-bells and Canterbury-bells," said Hare.

"I might make a bell," said the Mole, holding the penny in his strong hands. "I will bend it and bend it and twist it with my fingers till –"

And he walked musingly out of the house.

"GOOD NIGHT, GOOD-NIGHT," everyone called after him, but he only said, "And bend it and twist it and bend it," as he went slowly down the garden path with the moonlight on his silver penny.

HARE TOOK THE BOOK OF riddles to bed with him, and prepared to astonish Squirrel with a joke.

But when he awoke without his A-tishoo, he felt so grateful to Grey Rabbit that he got up early, and went out into the fields to look for bells.

WHEN GREY RABBIT HAD FILLED the little blue-rimmed mugs with milk, she called Hare:

"Hare, Hare, come to breakfast."

Hare came scampering in.

"I'm going to the village shop to get that bell," announced Squirrel.

"Oh, Squirrel!" exclaimed Grey Rabbit, "please don't. The old woman might catch you."

After dinner, when the old woman had her nap, Squirrel started off. She put on her best yellow dress, and her little blue shoes, and she tied her tail with a bow of blue ribbon.

S HE RAN WITH A HOP AND A SKIP
down the lane, leaping over budding
brambles. She entered the village, and
found all quiet. She ran swiftly across the
empty market-place to the shop, but the
door was shut, so she hid in a garden.

Presently a woman came out of a cottage and pushed open the shop door.
Tinkle, Tinkle, went the bell.

"It's still there!" said Squirrel.

"A pound of candles, please, Mrs Bunting," said the woman.

As Mrs Bunting reached for the candles the Squirrel leapt at the bell, and tugged and bit and pushed.

The two women shrieked as the jangling bell banged violently backwards and forwards with a yellow animal swinging on it, and they both ran screaming to the Blacksmith next door.

SQUIRREL KICKED HER SHOES OFF and lost her blue bow, but she forced the bell, and fell with it to the floor, knocking over three buckets, a milkcan, a mouse-trap, and a basket of eggs. Such a din and clatter came from the shop! Squirrel picked up the bell and ran out of the door, jingling-jangling through the market-place.

"There it is, there it is, Mr Blacksmith. That's the creature and it's got my bell," cried Mrs Bunting.

THE BLACKSMITH THREW A hammer after Squirrel which hit the bell, making it ring even more.

"My daughters will say it was another rabbit, when they come home," said Mrs Bunting angrily.

"It's my opinion it was a Squirrel, ma'am," said the Blacksmith mildly.

Away went Squirrel, dragging the noisy bell with its coil of thick springs twisting round her tail. Such a rattle was never heard, and the dogs and the cats awoke, barking and howling.

SHE PASSED THE OLD BROWN
mare, who shied in a fright and
nearly upset the farmer out of the cart.
She banged and bumped along the road,
up the lane, through the garden, and into
the house.

Squirrel was a heroine that day.

But when Hare and Grey Rabbit
dragged the bell across the Wood to Wise
Owl's door, he put out his head with half-
shut eyes and hooted.

"Who's waking up all the Wood? How
can I catch any dinner with that
hullabaloo? How can I sleep with that

Jingle-jangle? Take it away!" And he banged his door, so that the little white tail shook.

They left the bell to rust in the Wood, and ages afterwards it was found by a gamekeeper, who returned it to Mrs Bunting.

When the dejected Hare and Grey Rabbit got home they found Mole talking to Squirrel. He had brought a silver bell, a little bigger than a Hare-bell, a little less than a Foxglove-bell, with a tiny clapper of a hawthorn stone, hung on a hair from a white mare's tail.

WHEN HE SHOOK IT A SWEET silvery tinkle came from it, so delicate, so thin, so musical, that Squirrel and Hare looked round to see if a Jenny Wren was in the room, and Grey Rabbit looked out to see if the stars were singing.

All round the bell Moldy Warp had made a pattern of lines like a shell, and in the middle the eagle spread his wings. They hung up the bell by its twist of sheep's wool, and listened to the song of bees and flowers and rippling sunny leaves, and deep moss which it sang to them.

GREY RABBIT STARTED OFF WITH it as soon as it was dusk. She felt no fear as she carried it through the Wood, for the Wood held its breath to listen.

"What is that?" asked Wise Owl, as he peered down from his branch.

"A bell for my tail," said Grey Rabbit boldly, and she tinkled the little silver bell.

Owl climbed down. "You shall have your tail, Grey Rabbit. Give me the bell. It is soft," he went on; "It is beautiful, for it is like a flower. It is wise, for it lived in the beginning of the world."

So he hung up the bell on his front door, and there it sang with every breeze. And he gave Grey Rabbit her soft white tail in exchange. He fastened it on with threads of Stitch-wort, and anointed it with the Herb of St John, so that by the time Grey Rabbit reached home again her tail was as good as ever.

But Moldy Warp took with him to his house under the green fields a bottle of Primrose Wine and the thanks of the little company.

William Heinemann Ltd
Michelin House
81, Fulham Road, London SW3 6RB

LONDON · MELBOURNE · AUCKLAND

Text and illustrations copyright © William Heinemann 1930
First published 1930
This edition published 1992
ISBN 434 96927 3
Produced by Mandarin
Printed and bound in Hong Kong